JOURNEY TO THE CENTRE OF THE ONION

Allen Ashley

Journey to the Centre of the Onion
by Allen Ashley
ISBN: 978-1-913766-11-5

Cover Art by David Rix

Publication Date: June 2023

All text copyright 2023 Allen Ashley

TOWARDS

The onion was at the centre of all meals in our village and the monument in the central square reflected this preoccupation. Some four metres wide as an average measurement for a not perfectly symmetrical – and therefore, size apart, realistic – depiction. The Great Bulb was held in place by several taut wires. This gave it the appearance from certain angles or in certain nocturnal settings of floating in space. Unsupported. Hovering like something celestial come down to – or maybe attempting to return to – Earth.

It's big-headed of me to say so but our island culture is the most developed in the known world. It is we who are pushing forwards the boundaries of knowledge, culture, human activity and behaviour.

The inferior inhabitants of neighbouring settlements had a terrible habit of wafting their hands in front of their noses whenever they passed close to us. Suggesting, of course, that our breath or body odour was less than pristine. How would we know and why should we care?

Out of all of the habitations spanning our glorious land, only our village boasted an all-ages school that had departments in natural philosophy, practical science and our world-renowned academy for the study and propagation of root vegetables and edible tubers.

But we were not stopping there. The urge to investigate, to explore, to know was as strong in us as sunlight acting upon chlorophyll.

"Of course," Violet said, "some say that the question of how many layers there are to an onion can be answered in the same way as: how many sides are there to a circle?"

I was aware of her disappointment at not being chosen for Professor Herbiage's forthcoming mission and I responded as kindly as I could. "That one is often counted as two – the inside and the outside."

"Likewise the onion. And everything else we eat."

I shook my head. "Even a child could count more than two layers in their palm or in the frying pan."

"You think I'm childish, Linden, don't you?"

I saw tears forming on her elfin face, as surely as if she were at the chopping board cutting into mountains of our staple food. "Nothing of the sort," I mumbled. "Listen, Violet, I didn't choose the crew. You can't expect me to…"

But she had departed. I stood a while pondering the Great Bulb as the first of the forecast raindrops spattered its surface. The monument had weathered extremely well and the slight acidic discolouration only made its outer surface a more naturalistic light brown shade. Other pigments had been available – green, redcurrant, off-white – but the earthy tone had won the day back when the statue had first been conceived.

○

The Great Onion, the Holy Vegetable. This is the abiding symbol and driver of our culture. Replete with sexual connotations: some see it as the vulva, some as the testicle, some as the head at the top of the penis. Likely the Onion is all of these and more. The mother and father of our vibrant culture, the beating heart, the evolutionary instigator that has pushed us to lately develop a broader range of sexualities. Without surgical interference but through natural selection. Leaving some of us – myself included – indeterminate or fluid. Sometimes exhibiting characteristics of both the traditional assigned biological roles or oscillating between one and the other like a beanstalk in the breeze. Maybe soon I shall settle. Or the voyage shall rid me of much… or all.

○

I had studiously followed the news and rumours of the Professor's planned mission for a couple of years, attending lectures and press briefings with a borrowed and somewhat out-of-date security pass.

I had made myself visible by asking questions about the physics of the voyage. The adapted submarine was always going to be, by necessity, larger than the onion ornament that it was intending to enter and explore. Herbiage assured everyone that what we saw in the village square was a representation, a dimensional intrusion into our quotidian world, but also the summation, the totality of the whole of oniondom.

"Have faith, young man," he smiled.

At that point my features were, to be fair, marginally masculine.

"I worry, sir, that faith is a rather scarce commodity these days."

"Then we are fighting for the restoration. Next query, please."

And now there I was having reached the mission interview shortlist stage. All the groundwork was paying off.

"You have been diligent, young Linden," Herbiage beamed. "Although your background seems to be in poetics and student theatre, I suspect that you know as much about this project as anybody else." He paused to remove a fleck of food, doubtless bulb-based, from his fulsome beard. "Do you mind me asking – are you an indeterminate?"

"Yes, sir, I am. It's been difficult these past couple of years not knowing which way I will eventually swing. At present, I am in a mostly male phase but I suspect that will be changing soon. Will that cause a problem on the journey?"

"I don't see why it should. We are blessed on these shores that a sizeable proportion of our populace has the capacity – in their younger days – to experience both genders; or should I say travel the range of possibilities? Some say it is down to our copious consumption of blessed onions or the benevolent influence of the Great Bulb itself. Maybe our expedition will shed some light on this mystery."

"Thank you, Professor; it's not always that one finds the older generation to be so understanding."

He twiddled with a knot of his dark brown facial hair, looking for all the world like a contemplative tree god. "Let's just say that I haven't always been this way," he muttered.

◯

Some detractors have said that I have cashed in on my fluid and indeterminate state. There is some truth in that assertion. My volumes *In Transit* and *Between Man and Woman* articulate my experiences and have chimed with, or at least intrigued, thousands of literate readers and listeners. Indeed, it was on one of my foreign tours that I took the most advantage of my fame and enjoyed a string of curious young men and women who wished to spend a night or even a half-hour discovering a little more about my 'condition' up close and personal.

Violet is different. Our physical intimacy has been rather infrequent so perhaps I should believe her when she claims to love me purely for my mind.

Yet that is not always an undemanding or all-accepting love. We have fought at times and I have lost all of them. "Violet by name and violent by nature," she once opined. Our passion has a streak of rivalry attached to it. That is not a healthy state of affairs, I know. With each other's knowledge, we both applied to join Professor Herbiage's crew for the great mission to journey to the centre of the onion. We were both called back for second interviews for the post of lieutenant. On separate days.

Then one morning, I received hand-delivered confirmation from a royal courier that the role was mine. I knew that I was reaching the end of a masculine phase and would soon cross into female so maybe the timing of this expedition was not great. But, like so many things in my life, it was not by my choosing. I can be on top form as female or male but during the crossover…

I had yet to say a word to Violet. How would she react; and how would I deal with that reaction?

○

Violet settled a couple of years ago into female form. Somewhat elfin and boyish still but now beyond changes. I think I may eventually achieve something similar.

Remnants of her masculine stages remained. She retained a surprising degree of physical strength and prowess 'for a girl!' as she often reminded me.

We were at the annual harvest fayre and the barkers soon silenced themselves when Violet proved capable of winning prizes at every stall she visited. Archery? Bullseye. Coconut shy? Bowled over. Punchbag? Knockout.

I was keen to find a food stall offering fizzy beverages and something fried with onions but Violet's competitive streak led us to the *Trial of Strength* commission.

"I don't want to do it, I know you'll beat me easily," I said.

"Stop being a wimp, Linden. Swing the hammer and do your best."

My attempt was feeble, barely registering on the thermometer-like scale. Somewhere between, 'Are you a baby?' and 'Protein-deficient'. The stallholder was smirking, clinking our coins gleefully in his grubby hand. But when Violet swung and struck she made the top bell chime mellifluously and his mouth fell open like an expiring fish. To prove it was no fluke, she hit the target again. And once more.

The guy offered over a large cuddly toy.

"No thanks," beamed Violet, giving me a harsh squeeze, "I've already got one."

○

Professor Herbiage had conceived of his planned expedition about two years ago. His craft – the rather phallo-centrically named *Penetrator* – had required six months to build to his exacting specifications. The rest of the time had been taken up with local council meetings. Objections, requests for clarification, costing analyses, impact surveys... until finally he had received the go-ahead just a week ago.

It was now launch morning and despite their tavern-tattle of professed antipathy, huge crowds had gathered from the surrounding villages and even at this early hour, many enterprising locals were making good money selling onion-based soups, salads and sandwiches to the assembled spectators.

We would soon be, ahem, *penetrating* the Great Bulb and journeying to the centre of the onion.

○

And now here came the great procession barrelling down the hill with Professor Herbiage imperiously holding the reins of his horse-drawn carriage; the black and white steeds snorting foggy exhalations into the crisp morning air. Our mission vehicle rested somewhat precariously on the attached trailer. Ash, second in command, oversaw its safe progress with the calm assurance of a fairground barker walking the tilting boards of the waltzer in order to collect the fares. Bringing up the rear were maybe fifty or more strong men, mostly bare-chested and impressive from distance but probably goose-pimpled at close quarters. I worried that Violet might find their toned physiques more appealing than my more modest, natural contours. Where was she, by the way? Oh hang on, stepping down next to Ash as the parade came to an end – my elfin girlfriend but with her hair cut back around her thin white face.

"I've signed on as the cabin boy," she stated, smiling.

"The circus has come to town," I answered, giving her a brief but warm hug. Then I went to help Ash and Fern lift the Professor down from the carriage and help him into his wheelchair as he prepared to address the crowds prior to departure.

"Ladies, gentlemen, friends and curious children… by the graceful patronage of the school of natural philosophy, Lord Yam and Lady Holly, and the Regal Initiative for Investigation and Intervention," – this latter received a few boos – "I am pleased to announce that we are ready to embark…"

I zoned out at this point. I had heard the stentorian Herbiage recite this speech so many times in rehearsal; in fact, I had taken quite a hand in its precise wording. I was itching to go and would have preferred a quiet send-off or a final chance to check the provisioning aboard the *Penetrator*. But, I suppose, protocol had to be observed.

We were at the key moment when our faith and our belief in the Professor's doctrine would face the ultimate test. Empirically, the mission might seem a nonsense or a 'grand folly' as some of its kinder detractors had labelled it. The simple truth was that our magnificent metal and glass craft, designed and moulded at great expense in the manufacturing heartlands to the north, measured some eighteen and a bit metres at its pointed extent. More than four times the size of the Great Bulb, the onion. P into O shouldn't go. But Herbiage had contended and, to an extent, demonstrated that our village square onion was not just in and of itself but was also an embodiment of *all onions* and, therefore, easily able to accommodate our intrusion and passage because… well, are there not millions upon millions of onions extant in our world?

Doubtless there were many in the crowd who had come in hope of witnessing our catastrophic and potentially tragic failure. Others would be willing us to succeed, for this strange amalgam of science and magic to bear verifiable fruit.

… I was being called to step aboard. We would soon find out the truth of the Prof's theory.

○

In the western part of our kingdom, that which is most prone to tidal incursions and battering winds, the level of stratagems taken is determined by the pre-Equinox Ceremony of the Skin. For this biannual ritual, the local elders appoint three representatives from the young populace: a male, a female and an indeterminate. Each participant chooses one random onion harvested locally and determines the thickness of its outer, usually brown, skin. If the revealed skin is thick then it is certain that a harsh or severe Winter or a Summer of sea storms is on its way. If the skin is thin, however, then a mild season will ensue. A trio of samples is taken so that the result can be safely rendered as a 'best of three'.

Local and indeed national interest in this ceremony is particularly keen as all three novitiates are entirely naked so as to avoid any unintended contamination. Those lucky souls taking part often emerge with marriage proposals, modelling contracts or university places to compensate for their full-frontal exposure.

It's the closest thing our society has to a talent show.

When I was a child, I begged my mother to let me head off to the coarse western shores and become one of those chosen few.

"No, child, it's rude and irreligious," she countered. Or sometimes: "You'll catch your death of cold doing that. I won't be around to look after you."

And by the time she no longer was, my potential starring opportunity had long passed me by.

◌

We took our places aboard the ship. I was sure of my assigned role but I worried that Violet would not have received sufficient instruction. But she had been present at the majority of the original training sessions earlier in the recruitment process, so… Herbiage would certainly not tolerate any excess baggage.

"Well, crewmates," he beamed, "it's the moment we've striven for. I believe the submariners – whose technology we have shamelessly looted for this mission – have the expression, 'Batten down the hatches and damn the torpedoes'. I shall order those outboard to do their duty."

He flicked a switch and activated the intercom that connected us to the hordes outside. A great responsive cheer rose and fell like a breaker on the beach. He counted down from ten and at the nadir, we felt our craft lifted off its wooden trailer by the arms and hands of our mighty carrying party. Drilled to military precision, they positioned our great weight across their powerful shoulders and began a slow jog towards our target. As we closed to within a hundred metres, their pace increased.

From the front porthole, I could also see that a lone protestor had broken through the roped-off ranks. I couldn't hear his words but his placard read, 'Blasphemy' in bright, blood red letters.

"The fool, he'll kill us all!" Herbiage yelled.

Fortunately, our expedition had friends in high places. A mounted guard from the royal footmen – I couldn't quite grasp the non-sequitur there – launched a whiplash against the agitator. Who fell and was dragged to the side like he was entangled in a rabid vineyard.

We were almost at the moment of entry. Or impact. The Great Bulb filled our viewscreen yet even its immensity in proximity seemed still too small to absorb our craft. The brave souls carrying us parted to the sides like the bow waves created by a speeding yacht.

Time seemed to slow to the crawl of the flower head tracking the celestial progress of the sun. I was aware of the disparity of the reactions spread amongst the attendant crowd. Some were covering their eyes, others poised their fingers over the strings operating the shutters on their tripod-mounted photographic apparatus. All were anticipating something significant, whether triumph or tragedy. I was to be part of history; whether or not I lived to see the rest of the immediate future.

And then, almost without realising it – almost without feeling it – we were within.

INWARDS

And then suddenly we were in.

Through.

Had entered.

With no apparent ill effects to our craft or our crew. I squinted through the front viewscreen and our nose cone seemed undamaged. All instruments confirmed that our hull was intact and that we were moving forwards.

To where?

"We did it," Violet squeaked. "Oh Professor, if ever anyone doubted you they've got egg on their face today."

"Egg? I certainly hope not."

But he smiled, assuring my erstwhile girlfriend that he recognised the profligacy and potential inaccuracy of figures of speech.

For a moment, I almost desired that I had been in that crowd of gawpers, well-wishers and naysayers. What would their reaction have been when our lengthy craft achieved the seemingly impossible by burying and secreting itself into the Great Bulb? When vanishing before their beady eyes? Maybe many would pass it off as typical trickery, the sort of illusion one might expect from a bunch of onion-munchers in a society where five percent of the young people were hermaphrodites or androgynes or veered from one traditional physiological gender to another before finally settling. Believe what you see or be prepared to doubt everything?

I believed, I *knew*, that we had fulfilled the Professor's trans-dimensional promise, that we had entered a realm posited by philosophy and now proved by this glorious journey.

That was only just starting.

We sought the centre, the middle, the core of the onion, of everything.

We seemed to be moving; but through what?

"Shouldn't we have encountered skin? Or vegetable flesh?" Ash pondered.

"Stay steady. We will," Herbiage answered. "This is just the start. I would suggest that we have yet to enter the physicality of the one onion that is all onions."

"Then where are we?"

"One might describe our current location as being the surrounding aura, something like a protective force field. The sensation has some similarities with the attraction and deflection pressure one experiences around a strong magnet."

"Is that why I feel a bit sick?" Violet asked.

"I hope you followed my instructions to only breakfast lightly, young lady. We must stay steady. That holds for all of you. The monitors tell us we are progressing. Things will happen soon."

◯

People's curiosity wins out over shyness and near-strangers and half-acquaintances are always enquiring about my 'condition'. What can I tell them? At one and the same time it's a blessing and a curse. Mostly the latter. Sure, I get to experience the physical sensations pertinent to both traditional genders but most of the time I am in flux; and have been since puberty.

The changes occur nocturnally. Hence the redness of eyes and the somewhat washed-out complexion. It's hard to sleep when your testes are descending or ascending, your penis is emerging or your vulva is forming or withering. The move from one state to another can take a fortnight. And there have been occasions when the progress has stalled partway through.

Another factor is that one is never particularly well-endowed in either form. One presents as a boyish girl or a slightly fey young man.

Violet has seen me and been with me throughout many of these trials. Her time of indeterminacy was a few years ago and a shorter span. Of course, she possesses the experience to understand and empathise with my plight. But sometimes she tells me that I complain too much or other times she is displeased with the inadequacies and uncertainties of my physiology. I wish I had a big prick with which to satisfy her or pendulous breasts upon which she could suck all night.

As a people, we put a positive spin on indeterminacy. We are wiser in sexual politics, we are more open to difference, we are *advanced*. For my own part, my condition has powered my fledgling artistic career and I have fired off poems, watercolours and small ceramic casts that represent and interrogate my experience. These have brought a certain level of riches and fame or notoriety quite early in my life. I don't need the salary Professor Herbiage has offered me. But I feel now that I need closure, definition. Perhaps this great adventure will solve a few issues for me, help me settle. Every major voyage changes its participants, surely?

○

And then, almost without realising it – almost without feeling it – we were within.

Paper curtains. Thin, crisp and brittle. Browned off-colour by the heat or from hanging a little too close to an open fire. Crumbling all around us. Desiccating. What once was solid became powder. The decay of shed skin. A despondent slough. Fracturing into shards, behind us.

Almost like a snowfall. Or, more correctly, akin to ash flakes from a damped-down forest fire. I watched open-mouthed… as though to catch these light brown breakages on my tongue, to taste the part of the onion that is always discarded, always sent for composting.

"We should be through soon, shouldn't we?" Violet whispered and I shook myself out of my stupefaction. As much as I loved her, she had signed on very late as 'cabin boy' and I, assigned the role of lieutenant, should be setting a finer example of seemly behaviour.

"If you mean the skin, my dear, then I believe that we already are," the Professor answered from his specially-adapted seat by the main control panel.

And he was right. The peeling papery curtains had given way to liquid. This – sea? Channel? – seemed somewhat thicker and more viscous than regular water. But on the other hand, what did I know? I had never been in a submarine or even dived off a boat before. I'd been somewhat over-confident about my abilities during the formal interview for crew positions.

○

We once again faced a hard border that required our craft to deploy its frontal cutting equipment. The removed shards battered against our hull like grain husks in a drum but we progressed onwards. I was beginning to lose track of the passing of the hours. Our ship's chronometer told us that we had been aboard for two-thirds of a day but it felt like much longer. Perhaps time passed differently here and we would be wise not to set too much store by our instruments.

And what if a whole epoch had passed back in our home land?

○

Tendrils.

And more tendrils.

Although we had now deployed the retractable wheels as we were on a solid surface and passing through air rather than liquid, our progress was made ever more difficult by these stringy obstructions. The Professor despatched Violet and me on this occasion to be in the vanguard, wielding our blades like a pair of oversized scissor-ants.

"Clear a path," Herbiage intoned. "And bring in some samples before you finish. Their molecular structure will tell us much."

He had already told us enough. I wished my sword were sharper but it was very soon blunted by these exhausting endeavours. Violet cut faster than I, so I took the opportunity to gather a large bundle of tendrils in my aching arms, sweep them upwards like a harvest festival offering, and then wait until Ash let go of the wheel long enough to open the airlock.

"Spread them out, sonny." Sonny? I was well into my longed-for years of handsome maturity. "Now, let me see," Herbiage continued. "What are they? Fibrous, yes. Vegetable matter? Maybe. Animal or sentient – limbs, mayhaps? Well, time will tell."

"Do you need any more, Professor?"

Ash interrupted from the dashboard, "What we need is more physical effort from you. Your girlfriend's putting you to shame out there. Get chopping. Chop-chop."

As I dragged my bone-tired limbs back into the airlock, I thought I heard our pilot mutter, "By the sun, I wish I had a woman possessed of such strength as that Violet."

I would cut harder. I would find a way through.

○

Through a fluid section once more. This time, mercifully, Herbiage did not require us to swim outside our vessel and bring in gloopy water for analysis.

I had, though, rather enjoyed the sight of my lithe but curvaceous erstwhile girlfriend Violet floating ahead of me. I longed for our return from this mission when I hoped I could rekindle our forest fire and explore once again the contours of her thighs, the depths of her smooth buttocks.

○

The pessalisimus onion has always been praised for its sweet taste and almost perfectly spherical shape, which perhaps explains its vital role in the Ritual of the New Sun. This ancient rite has been performed by supplicants and hierophants – usually female; in fact, pretty much exclusively female in the patriarchally dominated division of roles – for many hundreds of bountiful crop-blessed years. Rite and happy outcome have become so intertwined that no-one dares question or break the spiritual link.

The pessalisimus onion, at one and the same time, represents our world and its wholeness, as well as constancy over time. Our orb spins and has always spun; crops grow and will always do so; if we can remain wedded to the right relationship with nature then we will prosper as we have done for generations.

A junior priestess lights the sacred flame. It is true, though not greatly significant, that the wax of the candle has a mildly narcotic quality which helps ease matters along. The outer skin of the pessalisimus is usually thin and brittle; the application of heat enables its easy and total removal without a great fuss.

The high priestess will have already fully disrobed. Now it is her task to peel onion layers away with her bare fingers and place them individually upon her tongue. All present observe her actions closely. It is not permitted for her to show any outward signs of scalding, scorching and the like.

The priestess becomes one with the onion, which is the world, which is all historical and possible worlds, which is the universal constant that sustains us.

Statistics show a spike in the birth rate following the annual Ritual of the New Sun and its attendant celebrations. To the dismay of many red-blooded, handy males, the working priestesses usually absent themselves for the duration in order to cool off somewhere quiet.

☉

Great tendrils again and we had to leave the ship to once more cut our way through these obstructions. The Professor called for further armfuls of samples.

"Cut carefully," he advised. "Be mindful of the correct procedures for specimen gathering."

Like we were collecting edible fungi from around tree roots on a sharp Autumn morning. Bring out your chair and raise your good arms to help us in this quest, you bossy bastard.

The last set of cuttings had self-petrified within minutes of being laid out on his dissecting platform. It was Ash's job to dispose of the resultant dust. Well-named for the task.

This time Herbiage was ready with his potions and his preserving fluids whose chemical properties cloak the natural sharp odour of the felled fibres.

I was glad of the physical training I had undertaken ahead of this trip. It was proving to be a hierarchy where brawn served brain. And all I'd hoped to do was to voyage and gawp.

And take occasional notes for my next collection.

○

My earlier masculinity has been left behind somewhere on this voyage. My hair is luscious, my hips curved and I pray that I am entering my final, feminine form.

○

Great white walls of yielding vegetable flesh. We cut, chop, desiccate with our rotors.

Through to another section. I am beginning to lose count
of the layers
the hours
the reasons
everything

○

Liquid. That would acid-burn bare skin and render taste buds incapable.

○

Strange ghost-like floaters. We have been unable to trap any of them to check provenance.

Animal, vegetable, mineral. Or otherwise?

Thin discs and platelets. The closest comparison I can find is the pale underside of the ray fish.

Maybe it's nothing, just a weird and random agglomeration of hydrocarbons. It's just our human nature to look for patterns and sense when, increasingly, there is none.

☉

Liquid again and the Professor required new samples in order to check whether the solutions were getting stronger as we approached the centre of the onion.

Ash and I were tasked with phial collection and I was not greatly surprised when he took advantage of the cramped airlock and made a play for me. In truth, as the voyage progressed, I had started to fantasise wildly and had begun to imagine our craft as a tongue tip unpeeling the layers of the labia. A seeking of a sexual paradise or a return to the womb. I wasn't sure.

I let him suck briefly on my breasts, like too many men had done before. For once nature had blessed me with something of an eye-catching asset. A year or so ago, I would have had no qualms about opening my legs and letting him fuck me for our mutual pleasure. But since I had met Violet, my wants and wishes had only been to further explore our shared femininity.

His penis was poking out like a gnarly-topped tree branch. I indulged him with one or two light-fingered caresses.

"Finish yourself off," I said. "And whatever you do, don't pollute the Prof's broth."

○

Liquid. Floating platelets taunting us. We are what you came to find. Catch us if you can.

○

But when we investigate outside, they are nowhere to be seen or found. Real or imaginary?
More likely, delusional.

○

Hours. Days. Apparent progress through the repetitive layering. Hard to believe it will ever end.

○

We had passed through so many layers that I had stupidly lost count. No doubt Herbiage was keeping score but, like the glorious sunny summer holidays of one's childhood, everything had rather melded into one somewhat timeless experience. My task was to recount the overall experience and its emotional, physical, psychological, physiological and any other ogical – maybe entomological – effects. Which I continued to do, filtered as ever by my own observer consciousness.

Violet had chastely put our relationship on hold for the duration of the journey thus far. I sensed that she felt that she had to prove herself and her place on the mission. As regards Ash, I still picked up vibes that he would have preferred both a more traditionally glamorous companion as eye candy on this seemingly endless voyage but also would have welcomed a standard male underling whom he could boss about or lumber with demeaning demands. We were the intrusion into the Great Bulb that is All Onions; I suspected that Ash might yet prove to be the fly in the ointment.

I really must stop mixing my metaphors or my poetry career would go straight down the toilet.

If we ever got home to recognisable civilisation.

☉

Eyes can hardly focus.
What is sleep and what is wakefulness?
The great walls we must puncture are smooth and white.
Her smooth buttocks.
Contours in the diving suit.
Expelling air bubbles.
Dripping glaucous liquid.

○

We have been overtaken by our primal urges. Even the disabled and previously asexual Professor has called out with a yearning and I believe I saw Violet leaning over him offering some relief.

I have no right to feel jealous. Ash's permanent erection has reawakened many of my old impulses. I love the way he leans away from his assigned station so that he can knock at or rub against me. Come here, big boy.

With the Professor focused solely on longings, he had not experienced since the accident, it fell to me to try and rationalise all that was going on. It seemed that as well as being the very epicentre of our cuisine, the holy onion was also the spur for our libido, the root of our urge to conjoin, to couple, to copulate. We were penetrating to its very essence and, concurrently, becoming uncontrolled expressions of its driving force.

☉

What is real and what is fabulation? There is only the journey.

☉

And at last Violet and I are freed from our employment bonds and any remnant of societal disapproval. We float freely together in what is now plain water, a joyous substance to wash clean our hearts and memories. We entwine like two mermaids, yet fully endowed with all that we need to coruscate our love-making. She is boyish, coy, sylph-like while my improved musculature will support us both. My body and my limbs are womanly and welcoming. Sorry for all the sorrow and heartache of past weeks. Our love is made strong by the certainty and constancy of the great onion that is all onions that is all of Earth and the whole of life, had we but already known it. Journeys are always within rather than without.

☉

A calm descended upon our crew. A return to normal. And yet there was one more small sacrifice to make.

Violet and Ash had their heads hunched over their respective instrument panels. I was the last to settle.

"Return to your post, please, Linden," the Professor commanded.

Was there a slight twinkle in his wise eyes as his mind catalogued all the surprises that this trip had delivered?

Tasked with quiet observation of a range of instruments and indicators, I had time to recall some of Herbiage's earlier teachings and responses to our concerns. That the effluent from our power source would pollute this universal basic foodstuff and render it inedible or at least unpalatable? No, the natural acids would neutralise any foul output. That our passage would create a rift in the structure of the Great Onion and all onions, which rift would be visible and obvious in all specimens? No, the plant would likely heal itself; besides which, our incision would not be detectable by the naked eye. That this very exploration was blasphemous and would bring down harsh retribution upon our crew and perhaps our whole population? Fear not, we have entered an age of scientific enlightenment and natural philosophy; are not our places of worship now merely maintained as sites of historic interest?

So engrossed was I in replaying these conversations that I failed to notice our current predicament. But Violet was on top of matters. I felt the urgency in her actions and demeanour as she revved the throttle over and over then slumped away from the controls.

"It's no good," she said, "we've stopped moving."

○

From calm to becalmed. To a frantic burst of activity. And continued failure to achieve our desired results.

Motors engaged. Wheels deployed although logically they would do us no good afloat in the viscous liquid.

All three able-bodied crew members sent out to push. Give it the old trawlermen's heave-ho and croak out a bawdy shanty while you work.

What shall we do with the becalmed sailors?

Leave them in the gloop 'til the rations fail 'em.

Early in the morning.

○

There is no sense of the diurnal in this predicament. The numbers displayed by our chronometer are meaningless glyphs from a long-forgotten language.

We will be stuck here forever.

○

The platelets glide past the viewscreen. So there is some movement here, some sort of current.

They are agglomerations of minerals.

They are flat-faced monsters circling like two-dimensional sharks.

○

A check and a re-check of instruments and functions. Everything is working perfectly. Except it's not achieving anything.

Motionless marooned mariners.

○

"We should never have undertaken this mission," Ash said. "We have gone against the laws of nature. We have gone against the divine."

"And what is divine, pray?" asked Herbiage. "The empty temples, the oppressive religious governance? The childish profession of faith and the trust in superstitious practices?"

"There are things in this world, Professor, that should not be interfered with. Not investigated, even. We have transgressed."

"Do you wish to leave our crew, Ash?"

"What, here and now? It's too late for that and you know it. You and your rhetoric have brought us all to our doom."

○

In the stuffy silence that followed, Ash's insubordination hung like a proverbial cloud in the middle of the control deck, polluting our mood and souring the success of the mission so far. Violet and I were on high alert in case angry words translated into action. Instinctively, we were siding with the Professor. To paraphrase that old axiom, he had got us into this mess so he would get us out of it.

At last, Herbiage spoke again:

"I trained under a great philosophical master on the mainland. He was much exercised by the conundrum of the observer."

"What do you mean?" Violet prompted.

"It has long been argued as to whether one can ever objectively observe any event – physical, emotional, psychological, whatever. Contrariwise, if an event remains unobserved, can it be said to have actually happened?"

"I know that one," I piped up. "If a tree falls in a forest but no-one is around to hear it, did it fall soundlessly?"

"Thank you, Linden. My great teacher, Mr Heisen, was of the opinion that all observation influences action, that by looking or listening we are interfering with and subtly changing what goes on. Impartiality is a myth."

"All very fine, Prof," Ash responded, "but where does that leave us?"

"Armed with this knowledge, we must always proceed on the basis that even our apparently passive observation is an active act. We must amend our activities, expectations and interactions accordingly."

○

We let his words hang for a while. Like our craft was hanging in this barely substantial nothingness.

○

We remained floating in this watery hinterland… Our attention torn between continual re-checking of our instruments just in case there had been a change that would offer us the merest glimmer… and the gazing out into the liquid that arrested us in both regular senses of the word.

Violet was worried about how long our rations might last. I answered her that if it came to it we could *just perhaps* swim back the way we came and hack off chunks of onion flesh. For water: we could probably filter some of the gallons of the stuff surrounding us.

○

Dull doldrums. Going nowhere.

○

"The key element is to minimise as far as possible our interference as observers," the Professor opined.

Herbiage was right, of course, but there were many other elements to the observer conundrum. And how are we changed by what we observe? In fact, surely that is an inevitable part of our existence? The things we see, hear and otherwise experience affect our psychology, our character, our thinking and our present and future course just as much as the direct physical actions upon our body.

REWARDS

As much as my nerves were on edge waiting for that longed-for moment when the pontificating and pondering Professor came up with a solution, my thoughts were also greatly exercised by Ash's recent outburst. I had not had him down as a religiously inclined retrogressive. Indeed, if he truly felt that way, he would have been amongst the protestors accusing us of blasphemy. But it seemed that under great stress his true colours had come out.

Which left me wondering what buried trait in myself I might yet unconsciously uncover.

○

"As far as possible," the Professor said, "we must seek to minimise our interference as observers. That is the key."

Heard that one before, Prof. Change the template, please.

○

The onions that grow on our island are superior to any produced elsewhere in the world. Obviously. A combination of soil acidity and compositional specifics, a temperate though variable climate, and years of horticultural manipulation have raised our regal vegetable to its paramount position.

Detractors – usually spies from jealous foreign courts eager to steal our cultivating and culinary secrets and expertise – these detractors have accused us of worshipping the onion as some sort of deity. This is to completely and deliberately misunderstand our actions and conventions. We have *ceremonies*. We *say* and *promise* a few things during those rituals. Where is the harm in that?

◦

"Professor," said Violet, "I've been thinking about the Heisen principles you spoke of."

"And?"

"You will remember that I was worried that our effluence would pollute all onions and our passage would lead to a visible rift in the multitude of earthly representations."

"Yes, child. That is all old ground. If it were an issue, we should not have progressed this far."

"I've got an idea I'd like to try."

Ash looked up from his control panel long enough to mutter, "Who made you brains of the crew, flower girl?!"

I wanted to hit him so badly that I could actually feel my fist cramping up. But I spoke calmly and said, "Come on, Professor, hear her out. What have we got to lose?"

○

At base, it was a simple notion. Yet one that fitted the Professor's theories like an egg fits a nest. Even Ash was cowed to silence by Violet's reasoning.

We turned off everything. All power-controlled motors, displays, air filtration. Even lighting. It was a bold and brave move; perhaps foolhardy, too, as there was no guarantee of reanimation should we wish to cancel the experiment.

At last we saw our surroundings with one hundred percent clarity. The most striking factor was that everywhere – the liquid, the distant walls of yet another soon to be breached layer of the Great Onion – held a greenish tinge.

The realisation made Ash initially gag and then begin moaning about corruption and poisoning.

"Shut up," Herbiage commanded. "This is the green of vitality. Of life, you imbecile."

I had a spanner handily tucked into the pocket of my cargo pants, ready for any outbreaks. Then:

"We're moving," Violet squealed.

And it was true. By whatever discredited deities our bad apple crewman believed in or by whatever combination of logic and good fortune, we were being drawn gently forwards. I had travelled in this submersible for hours and days that felt like months but at that moment I experienced a greater thrill than at any time previously. We were on our way but not under our own propulsion; truly, we moved as if by magic.

I must have appeared like some open-mouthed gawping fish staring out through the viewscreen as we sailed through the green-tinged water, onwards… to what? Surely another skin, another layer of obstruction?

And indeed before long we saw the whitish fleshy wall ahead of us.

"Deploy the cutting equipment," Ash ordered.

"Do no such thing," countered the Professor. "Everything must remain switched off."

"But we'll crash… and die."

"Use your faith now, young man. Trust in our certain deliverance."

○

Passing through folds of silk, light netting, webs that cloy and cling and yet soon are no longer there… a ripple runs across my whole frame… as if I winked in and out of existence.

Then we are coming softly to rest on an only-slightly yielding surface. Delivered. Alive.

I grabbed Violet and before I half-smoothed her hair with hugs and kisses I blurted out the short speech I had long planned:

"Is this the middle?"

Ⓞ

Ash and I were the first to exit the escape hatch. His pushing in front of me was a bother because I expected him to just stand and gawp at our surroundings. And then maybe fold his foal legs and adopt a praying position. In the event, he wandered off on his own a while, scoping the extent of this central chamber.

We were in a vast, vault-like space. White walls of vegetable flesh curved around and above us and had I been religiously inclined, I would have compared it to a huge cathedral. I wondered whether the unstable Ash would now at least feel satisfied that he had completed some sort of pilgrimage.

The air was still and odourless but not at all oppressive. Light was omnipresent rather than emanating from a single direct source. The overall atmosphere was one of peace and, although our craft was clearly an alien intrusion into this sacred space, at least the *Penetrator* was currently unmoving and therefore less disruptive.

"This is a sacred space," Ash stated, returning to my personal sphere as if he'd read my thoughts.

"Are you going to make a whole load more religious claims? Don't bother me with them. This place proves the Professor's trans-dimensional theoretical thingumabob."

"Thingumabob? I thought you were the eloquent one, Linden. Anyhow, I don't need to make what you would call wild claims, I can just relax here and bask in the glory."

Basking was usually reserved for corn ripening in a field or a lizard soaking up the rays to start its day. But each explorer is bound to put their own interpretation on the journey and feel that it's they who should get to have the new-found land for their own purposes.

"Truce?" I offered.

"Accepted."

"What happened on the ship stays on the ship."

"Absolutely. That's how it's always been for seamen… seafarers."

I laughed. "Don't talk to me about semen. I've had enough to last a lifetime."

He nodded. "You've settled," he said; and he was right. I felt lithe, sylph-like in my uniform. My breasts were more onion buds than the luscious hanging fruit I had rather hoped for but the gentle opening between my legs was warm, a mite wet and ready to experience intimacy.

"Violet will be pleased," Ash stated and at that moment I forgave him everything. We had been crewmates on an incredible journey, after all.

"The others will have finished the instrument check. Let's go and help them get out."

○

And now here we all were in the domed white amphitheatre of our hopes and dreams. The fates, the saints, the gods, the calculations had guided us here. Take your choice.

A further miracle: Herbiage had propelled himself out of his wheelchair and with just the aid of a long stick fashioned from our measuring equipment, was walking around like a conquering explorer.

History heads into the future as a game of rewriting, rebranding and reclaiming. No doubt future generations would query and question our aims and achievements. But for now I was in *the present* and needed no spectral glow to light my face with happiness.

"It's so empty," said Violet.

"This is not unexpected," the Professor answered. "That's the nature of the universe. The Big Bang, the heart of God and every living being or item… Yes, the centre of everything is empty. That's how it must be."

I gorged on awe, I filled up on wonder. I felt significant and insignificant simultaneously.

That we have undergone so much travail on our travels. That we had arrived at this revelation. The great zero, the great O, the onion that is much the same shape inside and outside, with its not quite perfect roundness that represented both the outer and the inner. Oh my, I understood that old joke only too well and indeed recognised it as containing the greatest wisdom. In its emptiness.

When the Professor indicated that it was time to begin what would surely be an easier, more *known* return journey, I almost said no, leave me here, this is home.

Almost.

But all homes must be left at some point.

Allen Ashley is an award-winning writer, editor and creative writing tutor. He has published with Eibonvale Press many times before, including the updated version of his celebrated Slipstream novel "The Planet Suite" (2016) and the anthology "Humanagerie" (2018) – this latter co-edited with Sarah Doyle and shortlisted for the British Fantasy Award. His poetry collection "Echoes from an Expired Earth" (Demain Publishing, 2021) was nominated for an Elgin Award. Recent projects include guest editing an edition of "Sein und Werden" with the theme "Animal Vegetable Mineral". Allen is the founder of the advanced science fiction and fantasy group Clockhouse London Writers.

www.allenashley.com